The Psychic

(A Murder Mystery of Sorts)

by Sam Bobrick

A SAMUEL FRENCH ACTING EDITION

SAMUEL FRENCH

FOUNDED 1830

NEW YORK HOLLYWOOD LONDON TORONTO

SAMUELFRENCH.COM

ISBN 978-0-573-69884-2   Printed in U.S.A.   #29653

MUSIC USE NOTE

IMPORTANT BILLING AND CREDIT REQUIREMENTS

THE PSYCHIC premiered at the Falcon Theatre in Burbank, California on March 26, 2010.

I would like to gratefully acknowledge Garry K. Marshall and Kathleen Marshall for producing the play and to Arnold Margolin for bringing it to their attention.

I had an amazing director, cast and crew and feel very fortunate to have worked with them.

S.B.

CAST

ADAM WEBSTER.........................Jeffrey Cannata
LAURA BENSON..........................Dana Green
ROY BENSON.............................Cyrus Alexander
RITA MALONE.............................Bridget Flanery
JOHNNY BUBBLES.....................Richard Horvitz
DETECTIVE NORRIS COSLOW.....Phil Proctor

Directed by
Susan Morgenstern

Stage Manager
Deirdre Murphy

Set Designer	Lighting Designer	Sound Designer
Jeff McLaughlin	Nick McCord	David Beaudry
Costume Designer	Prop Designer	Casting Director
Joanie Coyote	Anna McGill	Alice S. Cassidy
Technical Director	House Manager	Marketing/PR
Mike Jespersen	Joe Farley	Chelsea Sutton

Managing Director of the Falcon Theatre
Sherry Santillano

Cover Art by Chelsea Sutton. Thank you to the Falcon Theatre for allowing its use for this edition.

CHARACTERS

ADAM WEBSTER – A mystery writer in his early thirties
LAURA BENSON – An attractive woman in her early thirties
ROY BENSON – Laura's husband in his mid-thirties
RITA MALONE – Roy's sexy girlfriend in her twenties
JOHNNY BUBBLES – A gangster type in his late thirties
NORRIS COSLOW – An NYPD Detective in his forties

SETTING

Adam Webster's run down New York basement apartment

TIME

The Present

Act I

Scene 1: Early afternoon
Scene 2: The next day – late afternoon
Scene 3: Later that evening
Scene 4: Several days later – late afternoon
Scene 5: Later that evening

Act II

Scene 1: About a half an hour later
Scene 2: Several days later – early afternoon
Scene 3: Several weeks later – morning
Scene 4: A little later
Scene 5: A month later – afternoon

ACT I

Scene One

(*TIME: The present. Early afternoon.*)

(*THE PLACE: The entire play takes place in a somewhat dingy living room of a two room New York basement apartment. Painted concrete walls and an old water heater in the upstage right corner with numerous pipes running in various directions from the top of it make it obvious that this room once served another purpose, possibly as a laundry room until some ingenious landlord came up with the idea of renting it as an apartment. The room is sparsely decorated with a definite absence of affluence or concern. The front door is at upstage left center. When opened we can see brick or cement steps that lead to the street level. At upstage center and upstage right center are two large windows with two old shades pulled a quarter of the way down. Through the windows we can see a concrete wall. Above it we assume is the sidewalk. Several garbage cans are placed in front of the upstage windows. A cardboard sign rests on the upstage center window sill which we only see the back of. Below the windows are several low bookcases made of bricks and boards and filled with books and papers. At stage right is the door to the bedroom. At center stage are two fairly worn easy chairs separated by a small table. Downstage right is a small table with a chair that serves as a desk. A laptop and some manuscript papers are on it. Against the downstage right wall is a four foot tall bookcase with a printer sitting on top. Against the stage left wall is an old refrigerator, a non-functioning utility sink and a kitchen counter. On top of the counter is a microwave oven and a coffee maker with a glass carafe*) *that is about three quarters filled with coffee. Below the counter are a few open shelves containing dish soap and canned foods. Above the counter are two shelves which hold several coffee cups and dishes. The overall feel should be quirky, not depressing.)*

(AT RISE: At the front door, **ADAM WEBSTER**, *a young man in his early thirties and casually dressed in jeans, an open shirt with a T-shirt under it, greets* **LAURA BENSON** *also in her early thirties. She is smartly dressed, in a pale blue conservative designer suit with a blouse under the jacket, something that a very proper young woman would wear if she were going to interview for an executive job or consulting with a lawyer. She carries an expensive looking purse.* **ADAM**, *although quite friendly seems a bit apprehensive, not quite at ease with himself.)*

ADAM. *(gesturing)* Come in, please.

LAURA. *(entering and looking around)* You have a very…interesting place.

ADAM. *(closing the door)* Thank you.

LAURA. I've always found basement apartments very special. I'll bet with a fresh paint job, some different furniture, an oriental rug or two, it could almost be livable.

ADAM. I wouldn't be surprised.

LAURA. Maybe some louvered doors to hide the kitchen area.

ADAM. I'll keep that in mind, too.

(indicates chairs)

Now then why don't you sit there and I'll sit right here.

(They sit.)

Incidentally, my name is Adam.

LAURA. And mine is Laura.

ADAM. Really? That's one of my favorite names.

LAURA. How nice.

ADAM. Yes. Now first of all I need to know how you heard about me.

LAURA. I didn't.

ADAM. *(disappointed)* Oh.

LAURA. I was just walking by and happened to look down and I saw the sign in your window.

(rises and takes the sign from the window)

Interesting sign. "Psychic Readings. Twenty-five Dollars." It's done in crayon, isn't it?

ADAM. I'm planning to have a more professional one made, but for the time being, I needed to have something to let people know I'm here.

(Rises and takes the sign from her and puts it back in the window.)

LAURA. So I take it this is a fairly new endeavor for you?

ADAM. Well, uh, yes and no.

LAURA. Which is it? Yes, or no?

ADAM. Well, "yes" as a profession but "no" as an ability. I've been blessed with this gift for some time and I've been encouraged by a number of people to put it to wider use. Incidentally, I have some business cards. You might want to pass them out among your friends.

(From a stack of business cards on his desk, he counts out ten and hands them to her.)

How about ten to start with? Unless you need more.

LAURA. No, uh, ten will be more than fine.

(looking at one)

You made these yourself.

ADAM. You can tell?

LAURA. They're in pencil.

ADAM. Oh. Well, the early ones I made are in ink but then my pen went dry and I had to do the rest in pencil. I may have actually given you one that's half ink and half pencil. Well, then, shall we begin?

LAURA. *(sits and puts the cards in her purse)* Yes. Why not? I suppose first you'd like my twenty-five dollars?

ADAM. Well, actually that's probably not a bad idea. That way our brain waves won't be congested with any other thoughts.

LAURA. *(takes out three tens from her wallet)* Right. Let's see. I only have ten dollar bills. Would you have change?

ADAM. I believe I do.

(He takes the thirty dollars from her and puts it in his pocket.)

Okay, That's thirty dollars. You have five dollars coming back. So…

(He pulls out his wallet and takes out three dollars, the only bills he has in it.)

Here's three dollars.

(From the nearby bookcase against the upstage center wall, he gets a small dish filled with change and dumps it on the small table between the two chairs and counts out the rest of the money.)

And six quarters, and two dimes, and four nickels and here are ten pennies.

LAURA. *(takes the change and puts it in her wallet)* Thank you. You can keep the pennies. There's really no great use for them anymore.

ADAM. Are you sure?

LAURA. Positive.

ADAM. *(extremely grateful)* Okay. Thanks.

(scoops the pennies back into dish and places dish back on shelf)

Well, that's out of the way.

(back to a more professional demeanor)

So, now, just what areas of parapsychology are you interested in?

LAURA. Parapsychology? So then you're more than just a psychic. You're a parapsychologist.

ADAM. *(sits)* Yes. I was tempted to put that on my business cards but there was no more room.

LAURA. By any chance, you wouldn't have some sort of license or certificate awarding you that title? I wouldn't be surprised if it gave your crayon sign a bit more credence.

ADAM. Well, it might, but frankly having this special ability is not a calling that can be learned or taught. One either has it or doesn't have it.

LAURA. And you have it.

ADAM. Amazing, isn't it? Now why don't we select the process you'll be most comfortable with as we begin this journey.

LAURA. Can you be more explicit?

ADAM. Well, parapsychology covers many frontiers. The most popular is looking into the future to see what you might encounter down that long and winding road of life.

LAURA. Fortune telling.

ADAM. Basically, yes, but with extremely deep insight.

LAURA. I see. And some of the other options?

ADAM. Okay. As well as looking forward we can also look backwards. Maybe you'd like to find out who you were in another life?

LAURA. You can do that?

ADAM. Believe it or not, just recently I helped one of my very dear friends discover that in an earlier existence, she was sleeping with Attila the Hun.

LAURA. Did she enjoy herself?

ADAM. Not that much. She said he was an underachiever.

LAURA. I'm sure it's a fascinating area but maybe not this session.

ADAM. Well then, we could always contact the dead? I once connected with Ludvig von Beethoven.

LAURA. Really? He was deaf you know.

ADAM. Yes. As a matter of fact, I had to keep shouting through the entire session.

LAURA. I'm really not into dead people so I'll pass on that one too.

ADAM. Okay, how about palm reading? You really can't imagine the revelations I find just looking at a person's hand.

LAURA. Another interesting suggestion but I don't think we know each other well enough for body contact.

ADAM. Tarot cards?

(rises and crosses to his desk)

I have a brand new deck, never opened.

LAURA. No. Too gimmicky.

ADAM. Astrology?

LAURA. I'm an Aries. I'm a little too doubting for something that questionable.

ADAM. We're about out of options. Just what did you have in mind?

LAURA. Don't you have sort of a no frills, run of the mill psychic reading where you simply tell me some interesting things about myself? Although I know very well who I am, I often wonder if others see me the same way.

ADAM. You want me to tell you things about yourself that you already know?

LAURA. Yes. Is that so difficult?

ADAM. I'm not sure. We would be dealing in specifics then wouldn't we?

LAURA. More or less.

ADAM. So if I'm wrong about you I would come out looking like a total fraud.

LAURA. Most likely.

ADAM. It's almost like being on a game show.

LAURA. Yes, but keep in mind you've already won twenty-five dollars.

ADAM. *(sits)* You're very strange, Laura.

LAURA. No, curious. So let's say that's one wrong.

ADAM. I didn't start yet.

LAURA. I did.

ADAM. You're very unfair.

LAURA. Oh, my. That's two you got wrong. I'm more than fair. If you knew me you'd absolutely agree. It's one of my weaknesses.

ADAM. You have many weaknesses.

LAURA. No. Just those two. Being curious and being fair. But they're outweighed greatly by my strengths. So far three wrong.

ADAM. You're a tough cookie, aren't you? Maybe that's why you're not married yet.

LAURA. I am married.

ADAM. You are? You have no wedding ring.

LAURA. I just dropped it off at the jewelers to be cleaned. I've been Mrs. Roy Benson for six years. Okay, that's four wrong. Maybe try an easier direction. How about my favorite color. I'll give you a hint. It begins with the letter "b."

ADAM. Brown!

LAURA. No, blue. How odd. Very few people pick brown as their favorite color. But keep going. You're bound to get something right.

*(**ADAM** speeds up things.)*

ADAM. You own a blue car.

LAURA. White.

ADAM. Your bedroom is painted white.

LAURA. Blue.

ADAM. You have a cat.

LAURA. I have a dog.

ADAM. His name is Barney.

LAURA. Her name is Mildred.

ADAM. You were abandoned by your parents, raised by wolves and now you realize you've just been screwed out of twenty-five dollars.

LAURA. Congratulations! You got one right.

ADAM. I'm so depressed.

LAURA. Now, now. I'm sure you were doing your best.

ADAM. *(rises)* This was a stupid idea from the start. I'm no more a psychic than a rocket scientist which as you already gathered, I'm not. I'm basically a struggling writer just grabbing at straws trying to make this months' rent. This psychic thing seemed like a reasonable possibility but obviously it isn't. Look, let me give you your money back. Besides, I need the change I gave you for the Laundromat.

LAURA. No, no. Please. It isn't necessary.

(rises)

I never really believed in this psychic mumbo jumbo to begin with. I'm in the middle of having to make a very upsetting decision. When I saw your sign it seemed like a possible way to maybe clear my head and now I ruined your day, too. Maybe I should have just let you tell me my fortune. I'm sure you would have made it rosy.

ADAM. Yeah, but you would have known I was bogus because when I didn't see your wedding ring one of the first things I was going to tell you was that you were soon going to meet a very nice man, get married, and live happily ever after.

LAURA. Well, hopefully that could still be possible because I'm not living happily ever after with the man I'm married to now.

ADAM. I'm sorry.

LAURA. He turned out to be a liar, a gambler and a cheat. I made up my mind to leave him but…

(a beat)

ADAM. But what?

LAURA. He asked me to give him one more chance. He wants to take me to Paris hoping that with all the charm and music and romantic settings, we might be able to put it all back together.

ADAM. It would be nice if you could, wouldn't it?

LAURA. I don't know. I know he's having money problems and really can't afford the trip. But he seems so desperate to save the marriage. I can't make up my mind whether to go or not, whether it would really do any good.

ADAM. *(A beat as his eyes widen in fearful concern.)* Your husband's planning to kill you.

LAURA. What?

ADAM. I said your husband's planning to…

(stunned)

Oh, my God. Did I just say…What did I just say?

LAURA. My husband's planning to kill me.

ADAM. You heard that? I said that? Oh, jeez. I don't know why I said that.

LAURA. You felt something. You saw something. I see it in your face.

ADAM. No. No, I didn't see anything. I told you. I'm a total fraud.

LAURA. *(shaken)* I need to sit down.

(She sits.)

ADAM. Look, I told you I'm a writer. I write murder mysteries and I've been trying desperately to come up with a plot idea that hasn't been done which is almost impossible because basically everything's been done. And now for some reason I can't stop trying to come up with one. My mind keeps clicking over and over, plot, plot, plot, plot. Come up with something, come up with something, come up with something!

LAURA. You poor guy. It must be living hell.

ADAM. It is. And I can't seem to turn it off. So when you told me about your marriage being in trouble and your husband who's got money problems taking you to Paris, well I immediately began thinking scheming husband, Eiffel tower, body falling...

LAURA. How awful.

ADAM. It's horrible. That scenario has been done to death a million times. So please don't even think about it anymore. It meant nothing, nothing. I have no idea what your husband's intentions are, trust me. I swear I'm no psychic.

LAURA. *(looking at him intently)* Maybe you aren't. But then...

(rises and stares into his eyes)

...maybe you are.

(blackout)

End of Act I, Scene One

Scene Two

(TIME: The next day. Late afternoon.)

(ADAM, wearing jeans and a T-shirt, is with ROY BENSON, a man in his mid-thirties, wearing a suit and loosened tie. ROY is a good looking guy but in a slimy way. He is upset and pacing.)

ROY. I can't believe you told my wife what you told her.

ADAM. I know. It was awful.

ROY. When she came home and said "a psychic told me you were planning to kill me," I felt like a building fell on top of me.

(He sits.)

ADAM. It had to be devastating.

ROY. Devastating? Devastating would be a good thing. It affected me so severely I actually ran to the bathroom and threw up. How could you even come up with something like that?

ADAM. I apologize a thousand times and then some.

ROY. *(pulls out business card from jacket pocket)* Anyway, when I found your business cards on my wife's dresser I thought it might be a good idea to talk. Interesting cards. They're written in pencil, aren't they?

ADAM. Some of them. Just what did you want to talk about? If it's suing me, you'd be wasting your time. I haven't got a penny. And if it's closing me down, don't bother. So far your wife has been my only customer.

ROY. *(rising and walking towards ADAM)* Look, we both know this psychic business is just a lot of crap, right?

ADAM. You won't get an argument from me.

ROY. I just want to find out what else you told her, that's all.

ADAM. About what?

ROY. *(facing ADAM)* About anything.

ADAM. I swear, that was it. We were both kind of trauma-tized by the whole incident. I mean, it just came out of the blue.

ROY. That I was planning to kill her.

ADAM. Basically, yes.

ROY. And you told her nothing more?

ADAM. Like what?

ROY. *(walking towards **ADAM**'s desk)* Well, like, you know, *how* I was planning to kill her.

ADAM. No. Not really.

ROY. Or *why* I was planning to kill her?

ADAM. No. Look, why would you even pursue this? We're in total agreement. This psychic business is a bunch of B.S.

ROY. *(sits at the desk)* I'm just curious, that's all. Thanks to this little episode a seed has been planted in her head and just in case we need family counseling now, I want to have as much information as I can.

ADAM. I guess that makes sense. But I swear there was no rhyme or reason for it. There was no premonition, no vision, nothing. I just blurted it out. Like I told your wife, I'm financially flat on my ass and this psychic business was strictly a last ditch effort to try and make a few bucks and nothing more.

ROY. Yeah. But still you did come up with this murder idea. That's kind of way out there, wouldn't you say?

ADAM. Look, don't think I haven't been bothered by this incident. It's like I told your wife, I write these stupid murder mysteries and unfortunately my head is filled with some pretty awful plots.

*(**ROY** rises, picks up a stack of pages from the desk and glances quickly at them.)*

ROY. Yeah. Murder mysteries. Laura said that's what you do. Have you written anything I might have heard of?

ADAM. I haven't written anything anyone's heard of.

ROY. Well, don't give up.

*(smiles at **ADAM**)*

A lot of writers don't become famous until they're dead.

ADAM. Please, don't try to cheer me up.

ROY. *(hesitant)* So, you don't think a guy taking his wife to Paris to kill her is a good idea...I mean for a story of course?

(puts pages down)

ADAM. No. First of all ninety-nine and nine tenths percent of the time the husband is always caught.

ROY. Yeah, but what if he did it in a very unique way.

ADAM. Unique like how?

ROY. Like, say, if they were at the top of the Eiffel Tower and she accidentally tripped and fell off.

ADAM. First of all, it's impossible. It's all caged up so not even a bird can fall off.

ROY. *(a brief beat)* I did not know that.

ADAM. Well, now you know.

ROY. Yeah, thanks for the information.

(walking around the room casually)

Just out of curiosity...what *would* be a good way for someone to kill his wife in Paris?

ADAM. Well, there are rivers and bridges all over the... wait a minute. Why are you keeping on with this? Oh come on now. You're not really planning to...unless... unless...

ROY. *(defensively)* Unless what?

ADAM. Unless you *are* planning to kill your wife because frankly I'm having a little trouble with this whole discussion. Maybe there is something here.

ROY. Are you crazy? There's nothing here. Try to get this through your head. A husband does not take a wife to Paris, the city of lights and romance on a whim. I was going there for a reason. To save our marriage.

ADAM. I know. She told me that.

ROY. I know she told you that. And now I'm telling you that.

*(face to face with **ADAM**)*

Just be assured that I love Rita with all my heart.

ADAM. Laura.

ROY. What?

ADAM. Your wife's name is Laura. You called her Rita.

ROY. No. I said Laura. I know my wife's name.

ADAM. Yes, but you said Rita. I may not have talent but I do
have a good memory.

ROY. Rita, huh? Well, then I'm sorry. I meant to say Laura.

(*walks away from* **ADAM**)

You're doing a bang up job of getting on my nerves. As
God is my witness, I don't even know a Rita.

ADAM. Sure you do. You're having an affair with her.

ROY. What?

ADAM. I said you're having an affair with this Rita.

ROY. Oh, come on now. Is this another one of your asinine,
out-of-the-blue revelations?

ADAM. Not at all. I'm just following you down a very logical
path that leads to murder.

(**ROY** *starts to back away as* **ADAM** *pursues him.*)

ROY. Murder? What murder? There is no murder.

ADAM. Not yet. But there could be one, right? Admit it.
There is a Rita and you're having an affair with her.
Your wife said you had a cheating problem among
other things.

(**ROY** *finds himself backed up to the kitchen counter. He
moves to the middle of the room.*)

ROY. All right, all right! You want the truth? Here's the
truth. Rita and I…well, it started off very innocently, so
help me. One minute we were at a cocktail party with
our clothes on and the next minute we were in a hotel
room with our clothes off. You know how those things
happen?

ADAM. I never had that kind of luck. But the fact is that
you're in love with her and not in love with your wife.

ROY. Okay, I'll give you that, but I swear I was hoping Paris
might turn it all around for Laura and me.

ADAM. I don't believe that.

ROY. Why not?

ADAM. Because it's now become obvious to me, Roy, you are planning to kill your wife.

ROY. Hey, let's get one thing straight. I may be a lot of things, but I'm not a killer.

ADAM. Not yet anyway, right?

ROY. Right. I mean...Goddamn it! What are you trying to pull here?

ADAM. Look, Roy. Don't be a stupid ass. It's an easy fix. You love Rita, you don't love Laura. So you divorce Laura and you marry Rita. I can promise you Laura will not stand in the way.

ROY. *(sits at ADAM's desk)* If it were only that simple.

ADAM. No, it never is, is it? The money problems, right?

ROY. Yeah. How did you guess? Unless it wasn't a guess.

ADAM. Your wife mentioned you were a gambler. Gamblers do have a habit of eventually losing everything. No big brainer in these kind of stories.

ROY. What kind of stories?

ADAM. A guy who's in love with another woman and needs money so he plans to kill his wife in order to get it.

ROY. Will you stop with that. I told you I'm not planning to kill my wife.

ADAM. Here's the way it usually works Roy. Either the wife controls the money or there's an insurance policy involved.

(ROY quickly glances at ADAM and then looks away. ADAM catches his glance.)

Shame on you, Roy. You'll have to do much better than that. The cops will have you in handcuffs fifteen minutes after your wife is dead.

ROY. *(rising)* You are warped, you know that? I think we've talked enough.

(starts towards door)

ADAM. Let me warn you ahead of time, Roy. If anything happens to your wife I'm going straight to the police.

ROY. *(turns to* **ADAM***)* For what? You're the one with the murder idea. For your information, I planned the Paris trip before I met Rita.

ADAM. I doubt that.

ROY. *(mocking sarcastically)* I doubt that.

(normal)

Who cares what you doubt or think? Anyway, as of this minute the trip is canceled. How's that? You just beat my wife out of a trip to Paris. I hope you're satisfied.

ADAM. Maybe I need to go to the police anyway.

ROY. *(moving back into room)* Why?

ADAM. Just for the record. Unfortunately, there's always the possibility of an accidental bathtub drowning or maybe a hit and run. Between you and me the easiest way is to hire someone else to do it. But that could become a little sticky too, because then you open yourself up to blackmail from a third party. No, you're on the right track. It makes sense to do it by yourself. But now you're thinking if you're going to kill your wife, you'll have to kill me too. Good for you, Roy. Your thinking is very logical.

ROY. Logical? Logical is for me to leave and forget I ever came here. Let's get one thing straight. You're a self-proclaimed psychic with a crayon sign in your window, who admitted to both my wife and myself that you're a total fraud. So, even if you did go to the police, what makes you think they would take anything you say seriously? I gotta go. Laura said you charge twenty-five dollars a session.

ADAM. Yes, but in all fairness you didn't come for a session.

ROY. True. But just as sheer entertainment, you earned your money.

(Takes his wallet out from his jacket and puts three bills on the small table at center stage.)

Here's thirty. Have you got change?

ADAM. Yeah, but all in pennies.

ROY. Forget it. Keep it all.

(puts wallet away)

You know, I was really curious. I thought maybe you just might be an actual psychic. Someone with a true gift. Now I see you're just a nutcase. A stupid, crazy nutcase writer who doesn't know his ass from a hole in the ground. I feel so much better.

(He starts for the door, stops and indicates.)

Maybe if you put a wood burning fireplace against the wall over there, this place wouldn't look so dismal.

ADAM. I'll keep that in mind.

*(***ROY*** opens the door.)*

Oh, by the way, Roy, your girlfriend, Rita…

ROY. *(stops and turns)* What about her?

ADAM. *(looking away from* **ROY** *and into space)* You're not the only guy she's sleeping with.

ROY. What?

ADAM. I said, you're not the only guy she's sleeping with.

(surprised and confused)

Now why the hell did I say that? And I said it twice, didn't I?

ROY. Go screw yourself, you crazy bastard.

*(***ROY*** storms out slamming the door behind him.)*

ADAM. *(Crosses to table, picks up money and sits.)* I believe I'm turning into a trouble maker.

End of Act I, Scene Two

Scene Three

(TIME: Later that Evening.)

(ADAM is at the laptop typing. The door bell rings. He goes to the door and opens it. It's RITA MALONE, a very sexy looking woman in her twenties.)

ADAM. Yes?

RITA. Are you the psychic?

ADAM. Well, to be honest, I'm not really sure. I seem to have moments.

RITA. We need to talk.

(She pushes her way in and stops suddenly.)

You live here?

ADAM. I do.

RITA. Sort of depressing.

ADAM. You should have seen it before I hired a decorator. What can I do for you?

RITA. You told my boyfriend, Roy, I'm cheating on him.

ADAM. Rita?

RITA. Yeah, Rita. Rita Malone. What a horrible thing to do.

ADAM. I know and I'm really sorry. It wasn't very nice of me.

RITA. It certainly wasn't. Poor Roy. He went ballistic. He broke dishes, knocked down lamps, kicked furniture. I never saw any man so upset. Fortunately, I was able to calm him down and convince him you were way off base. I have the kind of a body to do that, if you know what I mean.

ADAM. Yes. I know exactly what you mean. Look, quite honestly I have no idea why I said what I said. I don't know what more I can do than apologize.

RITA. For what? You were right. I am cheating on him. It's a crazy thing. The last thing I wanted to do was complicate my life more than it's been. But a couple weeks ago I met this new guy Johnny. Johnny Bubbles. Neat name, huh? It started out so innocently. One minute

Johnny and I were total strangers standing in line at
Starbucks with our clothes on and the next minute we
were in his apartment on the kitchen table with our
clothes off.

ADAM. Things like that seem to happen to you a lot.

RITA. You have no idea. Anyway, getting back to Roy, when
I asked him who told him I was cheating he told me
about you. Well, I was very impressed.

(sits at his desk)

Outside of horoscopes and fortune cookies, I'm a little
too bright to buy into this hocus pocus stuff. But you
really nailed it. So when Roy was taking a shower earlier this evening, he always takes one before he goes
home, I looked through his wallet and found your
card. Very unusual.

(picks up a card from his desk)

I never saw a business card written in pencil. Anyway
I wrote down your address and here I am. It's obvious
you've got a gift.

ADAM. Look, for starters, I have no gift. As I explained to
your friend Roy and his wife Laura, I write murder
mysteries and I seem to be putting that kind of a twist
on everything. I swear I didn't have a clue about you
cheating with this Johnny guy but if I were writing a
story about all that I know so far, that's the way I would
go. On the other hand, maybe I just wanted to upset
your friend Roy. He's not a nice guy and I really don't
like him.

RITA. Well, to be honest, I don't like him that much either,
but a girl like me has got to look out for her future
and Roy told me that very soon he was going to come
into an enormous amount of money.

ADAM. So what do you want with me?

RITA. I need to know if he's on the level. If he isn't, I'm
dumping him and going with Johnny. If he is, well,
then for the time being I'll have to put Johnny on hold.

ADAM. By any chance did Roy tell you *how* he's going to come into this enormous amount of money?

RITA. Well, kind'a. He says some investment he made is soon going to pay off. I think it's some foreign deal. He says he may have to go to Paris for a few days.

ADAM. He was planning to go to Paris with his wife and then kill her.

RITA. You're joking, right?

ADAM. No. He's doing it for either her money or to collect on an insurance policy. I'm not sure which, but it definitely has to be one or the other.

RITA. *(somber)* Oh my.

(and then joyous)

Then he hasn't been lying to me. I'm so relieved to hear that. I've been lied to so much it's hard to know what to believe anymore.

ADAM. Did you listen to what I just told you? He's going to kill his wife for the money.

RITA. Yes, but that's basically a family matter, isn't it? It's a whole different issue. Believe me, you don't ever want to get involved in one of those things if you don't have to. My sister still won't talk to me for sleeping with her husband no matter how innocent it all was. So Mr. Psychic, I want you to look deep into your crystal ball or whatever you look into and tell me what you think I can expect once Roy comes into this money.

ADAM. Off hand, I would say life in prison as an accomplice to murder. God, you're just as twisted as he is. This Johnny Bubbles guy. How does he deal with your involvement with Roy?

RITA. He's extremely understanding. Whenever I get together with Roy, which is only three or four times a week, Johnny just waits in the coffee shop across the street until Roy leaves.

ADAM. The man is a prince.

RITA. Isn't he? It's obvious he's crazy about me. He doesn't know I know this, but he follows me everywhere like a puppy dog. Day and night. He doesn't let me out of his sight. In a way, it's very flattering. I've never had any man so concerned about me.

ADAM. *(unnerved)* Did he follow you here?

RITA. No. Tonight's the night he has to have dinner with his mother. But he makes sure I call him every hour on the hour to tell him where I am and what I'm doing. Well, I gotta run. Thanks for clearing up this Roy thing for me. Your sign says twenty-five dollars. This is my first time dealing with somebody like you. Is it customary to leave a tip?

ADAM. I wouldn't.

RITA. Okay. I'll trust your judgment.

(**RITA** *sits down and digs into her purse, searching for some bills. In the process she pulls out a powder compact, a hair brush and a gun and places them on the table.*)

If you don't mind, I'd like to check in with you from time to time to see if anything else has come up on your radar.

ADAM. Excuse me, but I believe that's a gun you just put down on my table.

RITA. Oh, yeah. It's Johnny's.

(picks up gun, handling it like it was nothing to fear)

It fell out of his coat pocket a couple of days ago and I've been meaning to give it back to him.

ADAM. He doesn't know it's missing?

RITA. No. He carries a bunch of them. He says in this day and age with all the street gangs running around you can't be too safe.

ADAM. Listen to me, Rita. If you don't want to end up in deep trouble, you've got to get away from both of those guys you're involved with.

RITA. Is that a psychic prediction?

ADAM. That's a common sense prediction.

RITA. I'm sorry but I gotta have something a little more concrete. Common sense is just a little too iffy.

(puts gun down and pulls out some bills)

Here. Twenty-five bucks.

(puts bills on table and picks up gun again using it as a pointer)

Maybe you should buy a picture or two to hang on the walls. I'll bet that might cheer up this place.

ADAM. *(picking up bills)* Believe it or not, I'm looking into a couple of Rembrandts.

RITA. Good. Pick something with fruit. You can't go wrong with grapes.

(puts the gun, hair brush and compact back in her purse)

Well, I'm outta here.

(She rises and starts for the door.)

Take care.

ADAM. Wait!

RITA. Yes.

ADAM. *(concerned)* I need to warn you. This Johnny Bubbles guy...

RITA. What about him?

ADAM. Someone's paying him to keep an eye on you.

RITA. No.

ADAM. Yes.

RITA. Is this a vision thing?

ADAM. It just got emailed into my head only seconds ago.

RITA. So...So then you're saying I'm a set up?

ADAM. Basically, that's what I'm saying.

RITA. And...And Johnny really isn't in love with me?

ADAM. I would guess not.

RITA. That bastard. That low life bastard. God, what's wrong with people? Isn't there anyone in this world you can trust any more? Well, that son of a bitch has had it.

(charges to the door and opens it)

ADAM. What are you going to do?

RITA. *(turning toward* ADAM*)* I've got a gun and I'm pissed. You figure it out.

(She storms out. ADAM *shuts the door and turns to audience.)*

ADAM. Jeez. I hope Johnny has a good medical plan.

End of Act I, Scene Three

Scene Four

*(**TIME:** Several days later. Late afternoon.)*

*(**LAURA** is standing at the desk reading the last of several pages she holds in her hand. She is wearing the same outfit. Her suit jacket is draped across the back of the desk chair. She sighs and puts the pages down next to the laptop. **ADAM,** wearing jeans and a different T-shirt, enters with a basket of folded laundry. He is surprised to see **LAURA.**)*

ADAM. Oh, hi.

LAURA. Hi.

ADAM. I was just at the Laundromat.

LAURA. I see. Your door was left open.

ADAM. *(sets basket down)* Yeah. The lock is broken. It's on my list of things to take care of once I hit the lottery.

LAURA. *(picks up pages)* I read your pages.

ADAM. Oh.

LAURA. Very interesting. It's about me. It's about you. It's about Roy. It's about what's been happening.

ADAM. Yeah.

LAURA. The bit about Rita and Roy. True?

ADAM. You knew he was cheating.

LAURA. Yes. I knew.

(a beat)

You used our actual names.

ADAM. I was going to change them before I submit it. Using the real names just helps me develop the characters better.

LAURA. In your first chapter where you meet me, I seem to come off much nicer than I remember being. I thought I was a bit bitchier.

ADAM. Yeah? Well, at first you did seem to have an edge. But by the time you left I think you mellowed a bit. Since it looks like you're going to be a very important person in this story I need to be careful not to make you unlikable.

(ADAM *takes the pages from* LAURA *and puts them back on the desk.*)

LAURA. Sometimes likeable people aren't very interesting.

ADAM. Well, it's only a first draft. I always go back and take another look after I'm through. But I think it would be very difficult for me to change you too much. I sort of like you the way you are.

LAURA. Which is how?

ADAM. Vulnerable. Sad. Conflicted.

LAURA. That's how I seem to you?

ADAM. Yes. Very much so.

(They look at one another for a beat.)

Anyway, I'm glad to see you again. I left several messages on your answering machine. After Roy's surprise visit I was very worried about you. There's no doubt in my mind now. He's planning to kill you.

(takes laundry basket into the bedroom)

LAURA. I know. I really misjudged my husband. I didn't think he had the balls. Does that give me too much of an edge to say "balls"?

ADAM. *(coming out of bedroom putting on a shirt over his T-shirt)* I'm not sure.

LAURA. Well, I'll say it anyway because I do say things like that. Balls! You might need to get to know me better before you're comfortable with that sort of dialogue. I'm really not the goody two shoes you think me to be or would like me to be. Believe it or not, I can take care of myself. If it will help ease your mind, you should know that I moved out of the apartment.

ADAM. When?

LAURA. A few days ago.

ADAM. I'm glad.

LAURA. Let me also clear up one more important thing for the story. The issue *is* the insurance. There's a two million dollar double indemnity policy involved.

ADAM. Really? So if something accidentally did happen to you, like Roy was planning for it to happen, he would get...

LAURA. Four million. Yes. You see, before we married, Roy and I each had inherited very sizable amounts of money. At the time, our attorney felt if something catastrophic did happen to Roy or myself, to protect the estate, it made sense for each of us to carry this large a policy. Unfortunately, due to Roy's less than virtuous lifestyle and his terrible judgment in the stock market, as well as the outcome of several football games, the estate is about wiped out and Roy is now up to his eyeballs in debt.

ADAM. What about your own personal money?

LAURA. I'm afraid most of that's gone too. I made the mistake of letting Roy handle everything. He assured me I was doing very well. After I left here the other day I did some checking on my own and discovered that I'm not very well off at all anymore.

ADAM. I'm sorry. Of course the obvious answer to everything is to cancel the insurance policy.

LAURA. I've already tried. It can't be done. The policy is set up so that it would take mutual consent to do that. If Roy is planning to kill me he'd never go along with that.

ADAM. Okay, then let's give the police a shot. I'll go down with you.

LAURA. That isn't going to work either. I called them. They said that until I was dead there was nothing they could do to help me.

ADAM. Yeah, I got the same thing when I called. Their lack of interest in preventive murder is mind boggling.

LAURA. But getting back to the insurance policy...

(*coyly*)

...it works both ways. If anything happens to Roy, then I'd get the money.

ADAM. Really. Well, that's something to think about, isn't it?

LAURA. It could be.

(There is an awkward moment as they look at each other.)

(changing the subject) I'm really curious about your story. It ended with your visit from Rita. If I hadn't shown up today, where would you have gone with it?

ADAM. In all honesty, I don't know. That's why I had to stop where I did.

LAURA. Would you like some of my thoughts?

ADAM. Sure.

LAURA. First of all, I would keep on with your psychic abilities.

ADAM. But I told you. I don't have any.

LAURA. Yes, but it makes it more interesting if you do, and actually at this point you're not that sure you don't.

ADAM. I'm sure I don't.

LAURA. Well, I'm not and neither are the others in the story. Anyway, from the pages you wrote I see all kinds of ways to go.

ADAM. Do you?

LAURA. Yes. Cruise ships are always fun. What if Roy takes me on a cruise and in an attempt to push me overboard, he slips and goes over instead.

ADAM. I like it. There's nothing like a good sea story.

LAURA. Yes, but where does that leave you in it? It's obvious you need to be part of it. Let's try taking it down another path. Roy does kill me but I come back to haunt him and he's never able to enjoy the money.

ADAM. I like that even better. A supernatural mystery. That always sells.

LAURA. Yes. But then again I don't see you very prominent in it.

ADAM. Do you really think I need to be?

LAURA. Absolutely. Okay, I think this one can solve all the problems. While coming to see the Psychic to find out more about the situation, the Psychic and I fall in love.

ADAM. And then what?

LAURA. *(slowly crossing to him)* And then the two of us kill Roy, cut his body up into tiny pieces, grind him down the garbage disposal, collect the insurance money and live happily ever after.

ADAM. I like that best of all. You can't beat a good love story.

LAURA. No you can't.

ADAM. Except if Roy's ground up in the garbage disposal there'd be no trace of him so how do we prove to the insurance company he's dead? And an even bigger problem is, I don't have a garbage disposal.

LAURA. Well, then we'll simply have to find another way won't we?

(They look at one another for a tense beat.)

ADAM. We're kidding, aren't we?

LAURA. Of course.

ADAM. I'm relieved.

LAURA. God, my life is such a mess, isn't it? And reading about it makes it even more so.

(She sits in one of the chairs at center stage.)

ADAM. I'm sorry. Look, if you want me to tear up the story I will. Like I said, I have no idea where it's going anyway.

LAURA. No. No. This might be the story that sells for you. Besides, I'm very interested now in how it ends.

ADAM. So am I. How about some coffee?

LAURA. Sure.

ADAM. Black?

LAURA. *(surprised)* How did you know?

ADAM. No other choice. I'm out of cream and sugar.

(**ADAM** *goes to the coffee maker and pours two cups of coffee.*)

LAURA. I've been waiting for you to ask me why I ever married Roy.

ADAM. That was coming. Eventually.

LAURA. To be honest, I don't know. He's not at all the kind of man you'd think someone like me would marry. He's wild, flamboyant, unpredictable, a bit crude... totally untrustworthy. Not my type at all.

ADAM. Maybe that's what attracted you to him.

(**ADAM** *hands her a cup of coffee and sits.*)

LAURA. Maybe. But it does confuse me that I made that choice. I guess it's true. You just can't figure out women.

ADAM. I'll try to remember that.

LAURA. *(nods thoughtfully)* Let's talk about you. Is there anyone in your life?

ADAM. No.

LAURA. Was there ever?

ADAM. Yeah. It's another very sad story. We were living together for several years. But then as in a lot of cases involving affairs with struggling writers, she had to make a choice between me and happiness.

LAURA. Maybe one day she'll come to regret it. Happiness has its own set of flaws.

ADAM. Does it?

LAURA. Absolutely. You stop looking forward to tomorrow getting better.

ADAM. Yes. That's true, isn't it.

(*Again they look at each other for a beat. There is something definitely happening between them.* **LAURA**, *puts the coffee down, rises and walks towards the desk and looks at his pages.*)

LAURA. Incidentally. I enjoyed your writing.

ADAM. *(puts down coffee and rises)* Did you?

LAURA. Yes. Your character especially showed great com-
passion.

ADAM. Thank you.

LAURA. There's a sweet innocence about you that's quite
loveable.

ADAM. Really. I didn't think I put that in the story.

LAURA. *(turns to him)* Now I'm talking about you in person
and not you in your book. You're a definite caring
person. That's why I thought it was a good idea for the
Psychic and the intended victim to fall in love.

ADAM. That's not at all impossible.

LAURA. No. No it isn't.

(a beat)

Would you do me a favor. I'm on the edge of falling
apart. Would you put your arms around me and hold
me for a bit?

ADAM. Quite honestly, I would like to do that very much.

*(**ADAM** goes to her and embraces her tenderly in his arms.
After a beat the two look at each other for a moment and
then kiss.)*

I think I'll go with that third plot of yours. Where we
kill your husband and grind him into little pieces.

(They kiss again.)

(blackout)

End of Act I, Scene Four

Scene Five

(*TIME: Later that evening.*)

(*The room is dim.* **LAURA***'s jacket still hangs over the back of the desk chair. The door bell rings. It rings again. The rings get longer. We sense impatience. The ringing is now accompanied by loud knocking and then angry banging which causes the door to open.* **JOHNNY BUBBLES***, a man in his late thirties stands silhouetted in the doorway. He is dressed like a typical gangster out of a 1940's movie, dark suit, vest, dark shirt, tie, and a wide brim hat. Now and then he puts a toothpick in his mouth that he keeps in his vest pocket. While tough looking, there is something quite likeable about him. He cautiously enters the dimly lit room. After several beats,* **ADAM***, trying to get his shirt on, comes out of the bedroom and switches on the light.* **JOHNNY** *looks around.*)

JOHNNY. Jesus you live in a real dump, don't you?

ADAM. Who the hell are you and what are you doing here?

JOHNNY. (*indicating*) Maybe if you put a pool table in here and got rid of all this shit furniture, it would kind of cheer this joint up. Anyway, I'm Johnny.

ADAM. Johnny?… Johnny Bubbles?

JOHNNY. That's right. Johnny Bubbles. Rita's Johnny.

(*Removes his hat revealing a very slicked back head of hair. He sets his hat down on the table between the two chairs.*)

You know, I should be a little more irritated with you than I am. Thanks to you, that chick almost killed me.

ADAM. I'm happy to see she didn't.

JOHNNY. I gotta be honest. I don't buy into any of this psychic crap but how you knew I was zagging the broad was good, very good.

ADAM. Zagging?

JOHNNY. Yeah, you know keeping tabs on her. Anyway, I've never seen any dame so upset. She tried to shoot me in the nuts.

ADAM. Not a good thing.

JOHNNY. I'll say. There I was just coming home from a delicious chicken dinner at my mother's, and there she was waiting for me holding a forty–five. Before I got the goddamn gun out of her hand, she put a bullet in my fifty-two inch flat screen TV and one in the mirror on my ceiling. Who the hell would have guessed she loved me that much?

ADAM. Not me.

JOHNNY. Me neither. She clawed, she bit, she scratched, she screamed.

ADAM. Sounds awful.

JOHNNY. It was the best sex we ever had. Anyway, she told me how she came to finding out I wasn't on the square with her. I was impressed. Very, very impressed. You obviously have some sort of, what are those initials where you see things, LSD?

ADAM. I think you mean ESP, although LSD might be a good second choice. Unfortunately, I don't possess either of those. I write murder mysteries and when Rita told me how you wouldn't let her out of your sight, it was pretty obvious to me what that was all about.

JOHNNY. You don't get visions or anything?

ADAM. Nothing.

JOHNNY. Yeah, but what about those other things she told me you came up with?

ADAM. Like what?

JOHNNY. Like how you knew this Roy Benson creep who she's dating was planning to kill his wife and about how you knew she was cheating on him with me. Come on, don't be modest. Maybe, just maybe, you do have a gift.

ADAM. *(apprehensive)* How can I help you Johnny?

(JOHNNY *sits in the desk chair, putting his feet on the desk.*)

JOHNNY. All right. Here's the deal in a nutshell. This dickhead Benson is into my boss for some major bucks.

ADAM. And your boss is?

JOHNNY. Fat Eddie Bistro. You heard of him?

ADAM. No. But I like the name very much.

JOHNNY. Well, Fat Eddie happens to be in the money loaning business with interest rates a bit north of insane. Sadly, our friend Roy, who as you know is having financial problems, had to turn to Fat Eddie for assistance.

ADAM. Which was a huge mistake.

JOHNNY. Of course. Especially when you miss a payment or two as Mr. Benson has unwisely done. If there's one thing you don't want to be, it's on the receiving end of Fat Eddie's very fragile temper.

ADAM. I get the picture.

JOHNNY. *(rising and walking around the room)* So one day Fat Eddie invites Benson to take a ride in the back of his limousine and with the aid of a heavy metallic object begins delivering a few choice blows to several sensitive areas of Benson's body as well as parts of his neck, pointing out to him his great displeasure regarding his delinquent payments and how the matter has now become a life or death issue.

ADAM. It's amazing how often a good beating is far more effective than a second notice in the mail.

JOHNNY. Exactly. Anyway, during this very intimate conversation, Roy somehow is able to convince Fat Eddie to give him a little more time because very soon he's going to come into a large chunk of cash and he'll be able to pay back everything.

ADAM. He was planning to kill his wife for the insurance money.

JOHNNY. Yes, which Fat Eddie seemed to think was a very
sound and reasonable solution to the problem. Now
the reason I was keeping an eye on Rita is because Fat
Eddie figured if Benson is stupid enough to try and
skip town, the girlfriend is the one who'll know where
he is. So that's how I got started with Rita.

ADAM. It seems it would make more sense to keep an eye
on Benson.

JOHNNY. Well, yes, but since the unlawful expiration of
one's spouse is frowned upon by the local authorities,
Fat Eddie didn't want to take the chance of getting
involved.

ADAM. It makes great sense.

JOHNNY. Of course. So here's the problem. Our dear friend,
Mr. Benson, has indeed, skipped town. He's missing,
his wife is missing and worst of all, Rita is missing.

ADAM. Rita? I thought you were keeping an eye on her?

JOHNNY. I was, but unfortunately I had jury duty for two
days. As you know, jury duty is one of the few areas of
government you can't screw around with. Besides, Rita
promised me she wouldn't do anything crazy. She has
no reason to lie to me. Since everything between us is
now out in the open, we're doing much better. In fact,
once this thing with Benson is settled, I was planning
to make our relationship a more permanent one.

ADAM. You mean, get married?

JOHNNY. Well, why not? Maybe it's time I settled down and
had a family. I think Rita would make a damn good
wife. The more I think about it, the more I realize I've
actually grown to love that girl.

ADAM. *(handing* JOHNNY *his hat)* Well, good for you and if
she ever shows up in your life again, my heartiest congratulations to the both of you.

JOHNNY. *(taking his hat and putting it back on the table)* Well,
that's why I'm here. Right now Fat Eddie is annoyed
with me. As you know, these days decent jobs are hard
to come by and I need to get back into Fat Eddie's
good graces again.

ADAM. So?

JOHNNY. So I need you to put on that psychic thinking head of yours and tell me where the hell they all are? Benson, his wife, and my Rita.

ADAM. I'm sorry, Johnny, but like I told you, I really don't have that ability. I'd like to help you, but quite honestly, I can't.

JOHNNY. Sure you can.

ADAM. No, I can't.

JOHNNY. *(pulls out a gun and points it at* **ADAM***)* Well, then maybe this will help you.

ADAM. *(backs away with his hands raised)* You're going to kill me?

JOHNNY. No. Just wound you in a lot of places you won't like. Now don't be stupid. Just concentrate. I know you can do it. I believe in you.

(The bedroom door opens and **LAURA** *enters.)*

LAURA. Is anything wrong, Adam?

(She stops when she sees **JOHNNY** *pointing the gun at* **ADAM***.)*

JOHNNY. Who's she?

ADAM. Good news, Johnny. You found the wife. One down, two to go. This is Johnny Bubbles, Laura. He came in on page 41 of the book.

JOHNNY. You're Benson's wife?

LAURA. As well as his intended victim.

JOHNNY. *(whistles)* She's a damn good-looking babe. What's she doing here? Oh. Oooh! I see. You two are having a little…

ADAM & LAURA. Yes!

JOHNNY. Good for you. Life is too short not to enjoy yourself. Especially in your case, Mrs. Benson.

ADAM. It seems your husband and Rita are missing and Johnny thinks I can tell him where they are.

LAURA. Maybe you can.

ADAM. You know I can't.

JOHNNY. *(once more pointing the gun at* **ADAM***)* I not only think you can I think you'd better.

(The doorbell rings.)

Who the hell is that?

ADAM. Well, if I was psychic I'd know. But I'm not, so I don't.

(The doorbell rings again.)

Do you want me to see who it is? It could be someone you're looking for.

JOHNNY. Yeah. Could be. Okay, open it. But keep in mind I've got a gun on you.

ADAM. Yes, but you're not going to use it. Not as long as you want me to find your girlfriend, which I believe is more important to you than anything else.

JOHNNY. You're good. Okay. Just don't try anything smart.

LAURA. You mean don't try anything dumb.

JOHNNY. *(turning the gun on* **LAURA***)* It doesn't matter. The message has been delivered.

*(***ADAM*** opens the door.* **JOHNNY** *stands nearby holding the gun behind his back.* **DETECTIVE NORRIS COSLOW***, a man in his forties, wearing a brown suit and tie is standing there.)*

Hi. Can I help you?

COSLOW. Are you the Psychic?

*(***JOHNNY*** approaches the door.)*

JOHNNY. Who wants to know?

COSLOW. *(stepping inside)* Obviously, I do.

(flashes wallet with badge)

Detective Norris Coslow, NYPD.

*(***JOHNNY*** immediately points to* **ADAM***. Unfortunately the hand he points with still holds the gun.)*

JOHNNY. *(indicating* **ADAM***)* He's the Psychic.

(COSLOW turns to ADAM, then wondering if he saw what he saw turns back to JOHNNY who has quickly hid the gun behind his back again.)

COSLOW. And you?

JOHNNY. I'm an innocent bystander just about to depart.

COSLOW. I'm afraid no one's going anywhere. Not just yet.

(COSLOW moves into the center of the room. ADAM closes the door. JOHNNY puts his gun away.)

Interesting place. You know what would look great in here? A skylight.

ADAM. This is a basement apartment.

COSLOW. Just a suggestion.

(COSLOW holds up a small plastic evidence bag with one of ADAM's cards in it.)

Is this your card?

ADAM. Yes.

COSLOW. Very unusual don't you think? It's written half in ink and half in pencil.

ADAM. It definitely seems to be an attention grabber. Now what seems to be the problem?

COSLOW. The problem is this. This card was one of the things discovered on the body of Mr. Roy Benson.

LAURA. *(shocked)* Oh, no.

COSLOW. Oh, yes. He was found dead this morning in an illegally parked car on Broadway and 72nd Street.

LAURA. Oh, no.

COSLOW. Oh, yes. His body was in the trunk. He was shot in the back of the head.

JOHNNY. An obvious suicide.

COSLOW. An obvious murder.

ADAM. Excuse me.

(He goes to his desk, sits and begins typing.)

LAURA. What are you doing?

ADAM. I'm writing this all down so I don't forget any of it. This is great. This is really great. Finally, this damn story is starting to move.

(They all watch ADAM *as he types away. Suddenly he looks up at Laura.)*

Oh, by the way. My condolences to the widow.

(He continues typing as the others look at him.)

(fast fade to black)

End of Act I

ACT II

Scene One

(TIME: About half an hour later.)

(DETECTIVE COSLOW, now wearing reading glasses, is pacing around slowly, finishing the last pages of ADAM's unfinished book. ADAM, LAURA and JOHNNY wait patiently for his reaction. As COSLOW reads he turns to each one individually.)

COSLOW. *(to ADAM. Smiling)* Mmmmm.

(to LAURA. Sheepish)

Oooooh.

(to JOHNNY. Annoyed)

Hmmmm!

(Finished, he sighs, puts the pages down on the desk and removes his reading glasses.)

ADAM. Well, what do you think?

COSLOW. Truthfully, I've never been a fan of murder mysteries. It's probably okay for devotees of that genre. Frankly, I'm more into romance stories.

JOHNNY. No kidding? I would have never guessed.

COSLOW. Well, I'm around mischief and mayhem all day long. When I come home I want to get away from all that. Now, my wife, she actually might go for something like this, suspense, thrills, excitement, something she doesn't get at home, but me, I'll take a Charlotte Bronte or a Jane Austen novel any day.

LAURA. Good for you, Detective Coslow. Clearly you're a man who's not afraid to get in touch with his feminine side.

COSLOW. No, I'm not. And I get a great deal of compliments for it too. Anyway, thanks to what you've written here, Mr. Mr…

(picks up pages again)

ADAM. Webster. Adam Webster.

COSLOW. Yes. Mr. Webster. I now have a much clearer picture of the details of this case and I must say it does not bode well for any of you. It seems every one of you had a reason to do in the late Mr. Roy Benson.

ADAM. I'm so glad to hear that.

JOHNNY. You are?

ADAM. Yes. It just proves that I've finally stumbled on to a good story. Lots of suspects obviously makes it more difficult to figure out.

COSLOW. Yes, it does, doesn't it? And this one seems very rich in motives too. There's you, Mrs. Benson with two of them. Motive number one, for the insurance money and motive number two, for being betrayed by a husband.

LAURA. I buy that.

COSLOW. Good. Now, our friend Johnny Bubbles here, well, according to the pages I just read, didn't he have a thing for Rita? When she disappeared with Mr. Benson, well, we all know the power of that green eyed monster called jealousy. It does have a way of bringing out one's uncontrollable rage.

JOHNNY. Hold on, smart guy. If I was able to find Benson, why didn't I find Rita?

COSLOW. Maybe you did. But for now let us deal with one murder at a time. And then there's you, Mr. Webster.

ADAM. Oh, come on. What reason would I have to kill that no good, low life scumbucket, who deserved to die more than anyone on earth?

COSLOW. One of the best reasons in the world. You're in love with his wife.

LAURA. *(surprised)* He is?

COSLOW. Isn't it obvious. It's all in the pages I've read. I can only assume you two have consummated the relationship?

LAURA. *(shyly)* Yes. But at this point it's just an affair. No one's spoken of love. Not yet, anyway.

COSLOW. Perhaps not yet, but the romantic side of me is convinced it's inevitable.

(puts the pages back on the desk)

Of course, another thought occurs to me. Being so deeply in love, as Mr. Webster clearly is, a man is much more bent to aid and abet his beloved's nefarious scheme of acquiring the very generous insurance disbursement that ensues upon her late spouse's demise.

JOHNNY. Christ, I haven't heard anyone talk like that since Masterpiece Theatre.

COSLOW. One of my all time favorites and a wonderful study in civilized behavior. I'm surprised, Mr. Bubbles you're even aware of such television offerings.

*(**JOHNNY** smiles proudly.)*

In any case, I have just outlined a scenario for three very good suspects.

JOHNNY. Wait a minute. We're not the only ones that could have killed that no good bum. What about my boss, Fat Eddie Bistro? What if he caught Benson trying to skip town?

*(**COSLOW** takes a small notebook and pen from his jacket pocket and makes notes.)*

COSLOW. Yes, very well. We shall add Fat Eddie to the list.

JOHNNY. And what about Rita Malone?

COSLOW. What about her?

JOHNNY. What if Benson decided to dump her? Wouldn't that give her a motive to do him in?

ADAM. Hold on. I thought you cared for Rita. Why would you want her to be a suspect?

JOHNNY. I don't. I just want to show this putz that he doesn't have all the answers.

COSLOW. *(again making notes)* Very well. I'll put her on the list too. So now we have five suspects. Is everyone happy? One last curious reflection, Mr. Webster. Documenting the events as you have, I wouldn't be surprised if you might have certain leanings or suspicions as to who our culprit might be.

ADAM. Believe it or not, Detective Coslow, at this point I don't. Of course, it's still early in the story, isn't it?

COSLOW. Yes. I suspect it is.

(puts away notebook and pen)

LAURA. What about you Detective Coslow? Are your instincts pointing in any particular direction?

COSLOW. *(sits in easy chair)* Let me put it this way, Mrs. Benson. I approach every case as a large jigsaw puzzle that requires assemblage piece by piece. Some pieces of the puzzle are big pieces and some pieces of the puzzle are small pieces. But whether it's a big piece of the puzzle or a small piece of the puzzle, one piece and one piece only, will be the one that completes the incomplete picture.

JOHNNY. Does anyone know what the hell he just said?

ADAM. He said that as of now he hasn't got a clue, correct Detective Coslow?

COSLOW. *(rising)* Right as rain, Mr. Webster. Well, I need to be going. I'm required to make a full written report of the incident and the paper work involved in a case like this is mind boggling. I'll most likely be dropping around again. I'm sure you'll have more pages for me. They really are a tremendous help.

*(As **COSLOW** starts towards the door his cell phone rings to the tune of "O Sole Mio.")*

Excuse me. That's my cell.

(He takes out cell phone.)

COSLOW. *(cont.)* I love that tune. It's so full of passion and melodrama.

(He hums a few bars with the music and then opens the phone.)

Detective Coslow. Oh? Oh? Yes. Really? Interesting. Hmmm. I'll get into it as soon as I can.

(He closes phone and puts it back in his pocket.)

Well, there's some more news on the home front. Miss Rita Malone has just been found dead in the trunk of an illegally parked car on Broadway and 72nd street.

LAURA. Oh, no.

COSLOW. Oh, yes. And what makes it an even greater coincidence, clutched in her hand, Mr. Webster, was your business card. What do you make of that?

ADAM. *(uneasy)* Well, first of all, I believe that now narrows the suspects down to four and secondly it seems that business cards are proving to be a very unwise investment.

LAURA. I'm so sorry, Johnny. This news about Rita must be very difficult for you.

JOHNNY. *(somewhat puzzled)* Yeah, you would think that, wouldn't you? But actually, for some reason it isn't and I don't know why? Maybe I wasn't as crazy about her as I thought I was. I wouldn't be surprised if I have a problem with relationships. I blame my mother for that.

COSLOW. Is that so?

JOHNNY. Yeah. In twenty years she's buried eight husbands. It's made me a little nervous about attachments. Funny though, I really thought I was nuts about Rita Malone.

(confused)

Apparently, I wasn't.

ADAM. Well, it's always better to find out sooner than later.

JOHNNY. *(thoughtful)* Yeah, yeah, I guess so.

COSLOW. Although in Miss Malone's case there is no "later" anymore, is there? Well, I must be going. Ta ta everyone.

(He heads toward the door.)

JOHNNY. Wait, Detective Coslow!

COSLOW. Yes?

JOHNNY. *(taking his hat)* Would you walk me to my car? Believe it or not, I'm a little nervous about these recent incidents.

COSLOW. Really? This request does not seem to be characteristic of you at all, Mr. Bubbles. It's obvious to me you have something more on your mind which is all the more reason for me to agree to accommodate you.

JOHNNY. Is that a friggen yes or no?

COSLOW. A definite yes.

JOHNNY. Thanks.

COSLOW. *(turns to ADAM and LAURA)* I absolutely love having characters such as Mr. Johnny Bubbles involved in a case I'm working on. It not only points out the various distinctions of class someone in my profession has to deal with, but it's also a reminder how necessary it is to look beyond one's very first judgmental impressions.

(He ends up facing JOHNNY.)

JOHNNY. *(a beat)* I'll bet your wife takes a lot of aspirin.

COSLOW. She does. Let us be off, Mr. Bubbles.

(JOHNNY puts on his hat, opens the door and starts out followed by COSLOW.)

ADAM. Detective Coslow! One more minute.

(COSLOW and JOHNNY stop and turn to ADAM.)

COSLOW. I'm listening.

ADAM. *(reflective)* It wasn't Fat Eddie who killed them.

COSLOW. Is that so? How do you know?

LAURA. Yes, how do you know?

ADAM. I don't know how I know. But somehow…I…I know. Maybe because it seems we all have better reasons.

COSLOW. I'll keep that in mind. Good-night.

(COSLOW and JOHNNY exit, closing the door behind them.)

LAURA. That was strange.

ADAM. What was?

LAURA. You more or less pointed the finger of suspicion at us.

ADAM. Yeah. I sort of did, didn't I? I wonder why the hell I did that. Oh, well, the good news is that you're no longer a married woman. And the better news is that I finally have more to add to the book. Not a bad day for either of us.

LAURA. Yes, not bad at all. Although I'm a little concerned about Johnny's need to talk to Detective Coslow in private. I wonder what that was all about.

ADAM. Yeah, that was a little peculiar, wasn't it? Anyway, I need to make some notes.

(He goes to his laptop and begins typing.)

Man, this story is really starting to come together. I think I finally have something I can sell, Laura. I really do.

(Standing behind ADAM, LAURA puts her hands on his shoulders and smiles.)

LAURA. I'm very happy for you, Adam. So very happy.

ADAM. I know you are.

(ADAM continues typing.)

End of Act II, Scene One

Scene Two

(*TIME: Several days later. Early afternoon.*)

(**ADAM**, *in jeans and a different shirt, is alone and pacing. He seems troubled. The doorbell rings. He goes to the door and opens it. It's* **LAURA**. *She is wearing the same suit.*)

ADAM. Hi.

LAURA. Hi.

ADAM. I haven't seen you for a few days. I missed you.

LAURA. I missed you too. But there were a bunch of details I had to attend to. I never realized how much paperwork was involved in burying a husband. I had to meet with lawyers, and the funeral director, the insurance company of course. It was very embarrassing.

(**LAURA** *hangs her purse on the back of* **ADAM**'s *desk chair.*)

ADAM. Really? Why?

LAURA. I couldn't stop smiling. Anyway, I felt you needed to be left alone to do your work. How's it going?

ADAM. Not well. I'm stuck again.

LAURA. That's too bad.

ADAM. Nothing seems to be happening on the case so I tried going several different ways on my own. I tried to pin it on Johnny Bubbles but that didn't make sense. Then I tried pinning it on Fat Eddie even though I know he didn't do it. That didn't work out either. I even tried pinning it on Detective Coslow.

LAURA. Oh, that's interesting.

ADAM. But that also went nowhere.

LAURA. What about me?

ADAM. What about you?

LAURA. Maybe try pinning it on me.

ADAM. That's not possible.

LAURA. Why not?

(He takes her in his arms and kisses her.)

ADAM. Because I love you. Why would I even think of doing such a thing?

LAURA. It's only a book. It doesn't have to be true. Besides, as Detective Coslow pointed out, I did have a motive.

ADAM. No. No, I don't care how desperate I am to finish this damn thing, I could never make you the killer. Never!

LAURA. That makes me very happy to hear that.

ADAM. Believe it or not, I'm toying with the idea of making it me. The problem is, once I killed your husband, what reason would I have to kill anyone else?

LAURA. What if you don't need a reason? What if you're just a plain homicidal maniac? And you can work the psychic stuff in it too. You can see yourself doing all the killing.

ADAM. Yeah. You might have something. How do I fit you in?

LAURA. Well, at the end you could kill me or I could kill you.

ADAM. And the reason being?

LAURA. Well, if you're the murderer, I could kill you to save my life or you could kill me because you think once I get my hands on the insurance money, I'm going to dump you.

ADAM. You would never do that, would you?

LAURA. Of course not. But maybe the thought might help take you in another direction.

ADAM. I'll think about it. I just know it needs a new twist.

LAURA. *(a more serious tone)* Adam, I had a visitor last night.

ADAM. Detective Coslow?

LAURA. No. Fat Eddie Bistro.

ADAM. Oh.

LAURA. It wasn't very pleasant. He wanted me to be aware of the fact that in his profession, the debt of the borrower is passed on to the family.

ADAM. And how much was that debt?

LAURA. At the present time, with his interest rates, eight hundred thousand dollars.

ADAM. Well, with the insurance money you'll be getting you can pay that off easily enough.

LAURA. Yes. That's what he'd like me to do.

ADAM. But?

LAURA. I'm afraid Fat Eddie is just the tip of the iceberg. In trying to straighten out Roy's affairs, I discovered he owes money all over town. If I pay off everyone he owes money to, I'll be left as poor as a church mouse.

ADAM. Good.

LAURA. Why do you say that?

ADAM. Because then I'd I feel on a much more equal footing with you.

LAURA. You don't now?

ADAM. No. I'm very intimidated by women with money or coming into money. I know I can never participate in keeping up their lifestyle.

LAURA. Do you think that was ever important to me?

ADAM. Why wouldn't it be?

(She kisses him.)

LAURA. That's why. Besides, if your book sells and you become a famous author you'll be the rich one and then maybe I'll be intimidated by you. I'll bet you'd like that better.

ADAM. Yes. Yes, I would.

LAURA. Maybe I would too.

(They kiss again. The doorbell rings.)

ADAM. Save my place.

*(**ADAM** goes to the door and opens it. It's **DETECTIVE COSLOW**. He wears the same clothes from the previous scene.)*

COSLOW. Good afternoon.

(Seeing LAURA as he enters.)

Ahh, the widow Benson. I thought I might find you here.

LAURA. Hello Detective Coslow. And how has the investigation of my late husband's murder been going?

COSLOW. Well, this morning we decided to make an arrest.

ADAM. Really? Who?

COSLOW. Fat Eddie Bistro. I know you felt he was not the killer, Mr. Webster, but all the facts seemed to point heavily in his direction. Someone who owed him money tried to run out on him. The consensus at Headquarters was that people have killed for much less. We were all in agreement that in the courts it would be a slam dunk.

ADAM. And what about Roy's girlfriend, Rita? How did you work her death into the picture?

COSLOW. Obviously a woman in the wrong place at the wrong time. It's a very precarious world. I can't stress enough the importance of caution one must exercise when choosing lovers.

LAURA. So, it's Fat Eddie Bistro. How wonderful. It certainly takes care of one of my big problems, doesn't it, Adam?

ADAM. Yeah. It's great it's him but it's not a very exciting conclusion for the book.

LAURA. Why not?

ADAM. I've never dealt with him. Not face to face anyway. I think the killer should be much more significant.

LAURA. Yes, but I don't think that will really matter if you make the conclusion exciting.

ADAM. How do I do that?

LAURA. Well, take a little poetic license. How about a car chase? People love car chases.

ADAM. And it's prompted by?

LAURA. Well, what if Fat Eddie takes me hostage and in an attempt to rescue me, you chase him in your car.

ADAM. I don't have a car.

LAURA. You'll rent one.

COSLOW. Oh, I like that. And then I'm chasing Adam because I think he's the guilty one, right.

(LAURA takes off her jacket and hangs it on back of ADAM's desk chair.)

LAURA. That's good too.

ADAM. Okay. A three-way car chase. What's next?

LAURA. How's this? Fat Eddie tries to cross the George Washington Bridge, but it's rush hour and the traffic is terrible.

COSLOW. Cars are honking and beeping. Drivers are cursing each other. It happens every day.

LAURA. Exactly. And now he's in the middle of the bridge, and the car can't move an inch so he gets out of the car and drags me with him.

COSLOW. She's screaming and trying to resist but it does no good.

ADAM. I like it. Go on.

(rushes to his desk and begins making notes)

LAURA. *(acting out scene)* He forces me to the rail. We begin climbing up grids and cables towards the very top. You follow.

ADAM. I do? I actually hate heights. Can I think this over?

LAURA. No. There's no time. You're there to save me because I mean more to you than life itself. You start climbing after us. Fat Eddie takes out his gun and begins shooting at you.

ADAM. He has a gun? You didn't tell me he has a gun.

LAURA. All gangsters have guns.

ADAM. Well, could it fall out of his pocket while he's climbing?

LAURA. No. But it doesn't matter. You keep on because you're braver than hell.

ADAM. Are you sure?

LAURA. Positive. We'll simply take more poetic license. Suddenly Fat Eddie is out of bullets.

ADAM. Thank God.

LAURA. He throws the empty gun at you.

(LAURA *and* COSLOW *mime throwing a gun at* ADAM.)

It just misses your head.

(ADAM *ducks.*)

And now on the very top of the bridge the two of you engage in a terrific fight scene.

(LAURA *and* COSLOW *mime punching.*)

ADAM. What about you?

LAURA. I'm off to the side screaming. During your fight with Eddie, I slip and end up dangling on a cable.

ADAM. Oh, no.

(COSLOW *puts his hand to his mouth in horror.*)

LAURA. I'm about to fall into the icy water below. It's sure death.

ADAM. I'll miss you.

LAURA. But just as I let go of the cable you grab me by my wrist. Fat Eddie begins kicking you.

(COSLOW *mimes the action.*)

In the stomach, in the head. It looks like we're both going to die.

ADAM. I hate when that happens.

LAURA. And then two shots ring out hitting Fat Eddie in the chest. He doubles up and falls to his doom.

ADAM. Wow. What incredible luck. Where did those two shots come from?

(COSLOW *raises his hand with glee.*)

COSLOW. From me! I do it all the time.

ADAM. Thank you. I owe you one.

(ADAM *and* COSLOW *look on in rapture as* LAURA *continues.*)

LAURA. And then with utter determination, you lift me up and take me in your arms. With the wind blowing in my hair and tears of joy running down my face, and with a magnificent view of the Manhattan skyline in the background, the two of us hanging at the top of the George Washington Bridge, and with our mouths wide open, kiss. The End. I know it's not original but it works every time.

(COSLOW *takes out a handkerchief and wipes his brow, obviously moved by her story and his total involvement in it.*)

ADAM. I like it. I like it a lot. I'll type it up right now.

COSLOW. Unfortunately, you might want to hold off.

ADAM. Why? It's a great ending.

COSLOW. Yes, but not quite the true one, if that's indeed what you want. You see, while we were totally convinced Fat Eddie did it, when we went to pick him up this morning we made two very important discoveries.

ADAM. Really? Well, maybe this might be even better. What were they?

COSLOW. First of all, Fat Eddie wasn't that fat. Second of all, he was found dead in the trunk of an illegally parked car on Broadway and 72nd Street.

LAURA. Illegal parking in that area seems to be a major problem, doesn't it?

COSLOW. Indeed. And what was even more bizarre, Mr. Webster, once more the victim had one of your cards in his hand.

(COSLOW *takes an evidence bag containing* ADAM*'s card from his pocket and holds it up.*)

ADAM. How surprising.

COSLOW. Think about it, Mr. Webster. Three people are dead and each one had your card in their possession. You have to admit that is a bit suspicious.

LAURA. But at best, nothing more than suspicious, correct?

COSLOW. *(returns evidence bag to his pocket)* At this time, I'm afraid nothing more than that. But still, a jury may find that enough to convict.

ADAM. Yes, that's true, isn't it.

COSLOW. One thing's for certain, the suspects are certainly thinning out, aren't they? I'm sure I will see you later, Mr. Webster. My investigative instincts still lead me to believe you know more than you let on. Much more.

LAURA. Of course he knows more. He's a psychic, remember?

COSLOW. Yes. So the sign in the window says. Good afternoon.

(COSLOW exits.)

ADAM. Damn it. I thought we had the ending.

LAURA. But we have the killer.

ADAM. We do?

LAURA. It's crystal clear, Adam If I didn't do it and you didn't do it, that leaves only Johnny Bubbles. Do the car chase with him.

ADAM. I don't know. It...it doesn't feel right. He doesn't seem to be as threatening as a killer should be.

LAURA. But you know it's him, right? You know he is the killer. It has to be him.

ADAM. I hope so. But I'm not sure. I'm just not sure.

(LAURA is concerned.)

(blackout)

End of Act II, Scene Two

Scene Three

*(**TIME:** Several weeks later. Morning.)*

(Adam's laptop is open and there is a page in the printer. **LAURA** *is at the counter stirring something in a metal bowl. An apron is fastened around her waist and she seems quite happy. She is still wearing the same skirt and blouse. Her purse and jacket are still on the back of the desk chair. The front door opens and* **JOHNNY** *enters and closes the door. He is wearing the same clothes.)*

JOHNNY. Hi.

LAURA. *(surprised by his visit)* Johnny. I wasn't expecting you. Adam just went to pick up a newspaper.

JOHNNY. I know. I've been waiting outside until he left.

LAURA. Oh?

JOHNNY. How long have you been here with him?

LAURA. *(proudly)* Six weeks. We're now officially living together.

JOHNNY. I see. How's his book coming?

LAURA. It's been a little slow. He hit a bit of a block again and had to stop. He assured me it's a very common occurrence among writers. But I think he's finally coming out of it. He was at his laptop this morning. I'm not sure how it went. I was still in bed. But when he left he seemed to be smiling.

JOHNNY. Do you like it?

LAURA. What?

JOHNNY. What he's written so far.

LAURA. Well, I haven't read what he wrote today, but I guess what I've read so far is okay.

JOHNNY. Just okay?

LAURA. Well, I'm not exactly on the edge of my seat. But then it's based on real people and real events and sometimes there's no real surprise in that. Especially when you are one of those people.

JOHNNY. But nothing else bothers you about it?

LAURA. Like what?

JOHNNY. Like us? Like how we function.

LAURA. Just what is it you're getting at, Johnny?

JOHNNY. You seem like such a bright girl, Laura. I don't see how you missed it.

LAURA. I'm getting a little tired of this cat and mouse routine. Missed what?

JOHNNY. Laura, you're gonna think I'm crazy when I tell you this, but I'm not crazy. We're not *real*, Laura. We're not real people.

LAURA. Have you been drinking?

JOHNNY. Listen to me. What we do, what we say, what we wear...

(pointing at ADAM*'s desk)*

It's all his doing. It's all coming from him.

LAURA. Maybe you'd better leave, Johnny. I need to be honest. I don't feel very comfortable being around you.

JOHNNY. Open up your mind, Laura. I loved Rita, right. I was ready to spend the rest of my life with her. When I found out she was dead, what did I do? Did I show any emotion? Did I tear up? Did my knees buckle? Did I act like I had the wind knocked out of me? No, I did nothing. And you know why?

LAURA. Because you killed her?

JOHNNY. No, because that's the way Adam is writing me, without feelings, without any genuine sensitivity. If I was a real person, I would have shown something. For Chris' sake, I lost someone I loved. Where the hell was the sensitivity? Where the hell was the goddamn sensitivity?

LAURA. Please leave, Johnny.

JOHNNY. Look at me, Laura.

(removes hat)

Look, at my slicked down hair, this ridiculous suit, this stupid hat. Who the hell walks around looking like this? And who the hell wears hats? But this is what he thinks a guy in the criminal world should look like.

(drops hat on small table)

JOHNNY. *(cont.)* It's embarrassing. I'm not a real person. I'm a goddamn gangster cliché out of the nineteen forties, using words like "dame" and "babe" and "chick." Goddamn it, maybe I got some rough edges but I don't need to have stupid edges. And the corny names he's come up with. Johnny Bubbles, Fat Eddie Bistro. It's like we're in a bad production of Guys and Dolls. And Detective Coslow, we're supposed to believe he's a New York detective. A guy so dignified, so refined, so immaculately tailored. Did you ever deal with a New York detective? They've got as much sophistication as a meatball sandwich and every one of them looks like they've slept in their clothes for a week. If Coslow belongs anywhere it's in the men's department at Bloomingdales.

LAURA. You're having a nervous breakdown, aren't you? That's what it is.

JOHNNY. Look at yourself, Laura. You're sweet, beautiful, well-educated. Why would someone like you ever marry a guy like Roy in the first place? Answer me that?

LAURA. I...I...You need to go, Johnny.

JOHNNY. No! No, you'd never marry a guy like Roy. Never! And think *this* through, Laura. You've been here six weeks.

(raises his voice)

Why wouldn't you be fixing up this shit hole apartment? Some curtains, some flowers! This is not the way you'd be living.

LAURA. Look, I don't know what you're trying to prove...

JOHNNY. Don't you get it, Laura. Everything about us is all him. He's calling the shots. Everything that's happened so far is because that's the way he's writing us and the bottom line is...

(yelling)

...he isn't a good writer!

LAURA. You keep this up Johnny and you'll end up in a psycho ward before the day's over. Please, tell me you don't really believe this gibberish.

JOHNNY. I can see you don't?

LAURA. Not a word.

JOHNNY. What's the use. I tried getting through to Coslow the other night but it didn't do any good either. I just wanted to warn you, that's all. Adam's got to end this story soon and between you and me, I think some more stupid things are about to happen. That's why I'm getting out while I still have a chance and maybe you should think about it too. I'm not ready to die because of bad writing.

(He takes his hat, goes to the door, then turns to her.)

I want you to know I did love Rita, no matter what Adam wrote. I loved her with all my heart and I grieve, I truly grieve. By the way, why are you always in that same outfit. Don't you have anything else to wear?

(He exits, closing the door. A beat and then the door opens and he steps back in.)

One last thing. In a million years, that hack could never write a scene this good.

(JOHNNY exits closing the door behind him. LAURA is confused. She begins laughing, hoping that might dismiss all that she's heard.)

LAURA. This is insane. This is absolutely insane.

(She takes off her apron and puts it on back of the desk chair where her jacket hangs. She looks at the clothes she has on, then lifts her jacket sleeve, looks at it for a brief moment, puts it back down and now realizes something is definitely wrong. She rushes to the printer, picks up the page in the output tray and quickly scans it.)

Oh, my God.

(She puts it down horrified. A few beats and then ADAM enters wearing jeans, T-shirt and an unbuttoned long sleeve shirt. He has a newspaper.)

ADAM. Hi, honey. God you'll never believe this. Guess who
    was in the paper this morning? Johnny Bubbles. He
    was found dead in the trunk of an illegally parked car
    on, of all places, Broadway and 72nd street.

LAURA. *(coldly)* Yes. I know. I just read your last page.

(He looks at her.)

(blackout)

End Of Act II, Scene Three

Scene Four

(TIME: A little later.)

(ADAM is at the laptop. LAURA is sitting on the arm of a nearby chair looking at him pensively.)

ADAM. *(not looking up)* You're staring at me, aren't you?

LAURA. It's true, isn't it? This has all been a manipulation, hasn't it? I'm not real. Johnny's not real.

ADAM. I'm real.

LAURA. *(rises)* I should have guessed. There were so many signs. Johnny was right. I never would have married a man like Roy.

ADAM. I don't think anyone will catch that.

LAURA. They'll catch a lot of things. You've left it full of holes.

ADAM. I'll fix it in the rewrite. I'm sure an editor will have some suggestions.

LAURA. You have to sell it to a publisher to get an editor.

ADAM. How could it not sell? It's got everything. Murder, love, greed, sex, plus a little comedy.

LAURA. So who takes the fall, Adam? There's only two of us left. Me and Detective Coslow. Who ends up with the short straw?

(ADAM doesn't answer.)

(heartbroken)

It's me, isn't it? And after you promised it would never happen.

ADAM. I couldn't help myself. I wrote myself into a corner. I needed some way to get out. I needed to do something special. And it makes the most sense. No one could possibly see it coming. No one. I'm sure of it.

LAURA. Johnny Bubbles saw.

ADAM. Yeah, well he's dead, isn't he?

> *(goes to* LAURA*)*

Come on, cheer up. Look, there's no death penalty in this state. With time off for good behavior, you'll be out in forty years. If I'm still around we'll try and pick up the pieces.

LAURA. You hack. You goddamn hack. That's like the ending of *The Maltese Falcon.*

ADAM. Good. I'll point that out. I'll have a better chance of selling the book.

LAURA. *(holding* ADAM *by the shoulders)* Think about it, Adam. You've never had anyone like me in your life, someone who loves you as much as I do. We could have it all. The insurance money, each other, the good life. Does having a book published mean more to you than living happily ever after?

> *(*ADAM *is silent. He looks away in guilt.)*

Answer me, Adam. Answer me.

> *(The door opens and* DETECTIVE COSLOW *enters.)*

I don't believe this.

> *(She goes to* COSLOW*.)*

I swear Detective Coslow, I didn't kill Johnny Bubbles and I have no idea what makes you think I did.

COSLOW. We found your business card in his hand.

LAURA. I don't have a business card.

ADAM. I'm going back to the beginning to give you one.

LAURA. Please, Adam. If I ever meant anything to you. Don't let it end this way. Please, don't.

ADAM. I'm a writer, Laura. Good, bad or indifferent. If I didn't finish the book I'd never be able to look at myself in the mirror.

LAURA. You rotten bastard! You got that from *The Maltese Falcon,* too.

ADAM. Well, at least you can see I read.

COSLOW. We'd better go, Mrs. Benson. Squad car's waiting outside.

(LAURA, resigned to her fate, gets her purse and jacket, looks around the room for a moment and then goes to ADAM and kisses him on the lips one last time.)

LAURA. Goodbye Adam. I didn't want to kiss you goodbye, but apparently you did.

(She walks to COSLOW who is now standing at the door holding handcuffs. He slips them on her.)

COSLOW. You might enjoy prison. At least you'll get to wear a different outfit.

LAURA. Oh, shut up.

(They exit leaving the door open. ADAM rushes to it.)

ADAM. *(calling after her)* I'll miss you, Laura.

(closes the door and sighs)

I really will.

(Lights fade to black.)

End of Act Two, Scene Four

Scene Five

(TIME: A month later. Afternoon)

(The room is basically unchanged except there are a pile of manuscripts in envelopes stacked on the desk. **COSLOW, ROY, JOHNNY,** *and* **RITA** *are waiting around. They are all dressed in the same clothes we last saw each of them in.)*

COSLOW. *(pouring himself a cup of coffee)* Coffee anyone?

RITA. I'd like a double mocha latte.

COSLOW. This is not Starbucks. It's plain coffee or nothing?

RITA. I don't know. I've never had plain coffee before. What does it taste like?

COSLOW. Forget it.

(He puts the pot down.)

ROY. God, it's so dismal in here. Do you know what this place needs?

JOHNNY. A bull dozer.

COSLOW. It's not the place that's depressing. It's him. Nothing seems to cheer him up.

RITA. Maybe he has a medical deficiency.

JOHNNY. Yeah. He already has a talent deficiency.

ROY. I think it's the book that's getting him down. He mailed out over twenty of them and within a month half of them came back rejected.

JOHNNY. He made a big mistake. He sent them to publishers with good taste.

RITA. Will you quit picking on him. He's doing the best he can.

JOHNNY. I know. That's what's so discouraging.

COSLOW. *(hears the doorknob moving)* Here he comes. Let's try to act cheerful.

*(**ADAM** enters wearing jeans, shirt and corduroy sport coat. He is carrying five large envelopes.)*

RITA. Hi, Adam. Anything in the mail?

(They follow ADAM to the desk where he puts the envelopes on top of the stack already there. He takes off his jacket, hangs it on back of the chair and sits.)

ADAM. Five more rejections.

JOHNNY. Good. The world of literature is still safe for awhile.

ROY. *(disappointed)* And we're still stuck here in Bozo's basement.

COSLOW. Perhaps we need to have a more positive attitude. Possibly that's all that's needed here.

ADAM. No. Johnny Bubbles is right. Maybe I am a bad writer. Maybe it's that plain and simple.

COSLOW. Oh, come on, Adam. You're being much too hard on yourself.

ADAM. You don't think I'm a bad writer?

COSLOW. Well, I wouldn't go that far.

RITA. Maybe you should start on another book. That might be fun.

JOHNNY. Not for anyone that has to read it.

ADAM. What's the sense of writing another one anyway?

(indicates stack of returned envelopes)

Look at this. Rejection, rejection, rejection, rejection. It's as if they couldn't get my book out of their office fast enough.

COSLOW. Now, now, Adam, good mysteries are very hard to write. Maybe you should start to think about going in another direction.

ROY. That's not a bad idea. Maybe think about one of those "How to" books. You know. "How To Lose Forty Pounds in Forty Minutes," "How To Retire At Age Six." People seem to buy those no matter how crappy they're written.

JOHNNY. What about this idea? "How To Write A Flop Novel." You won't even have to do research for that one.

ADAM. Hey, I'm depressed, possibly suicidal, and you're not helping matters.

(They follow ADAM *as he goes to an easy chair and sits.)*

Damn it. I miss Laura. I miss her desperately. Why isn't she here? When she was around, everything seemed so much more hopeful.

ROY. Forget her. She never wants to see you again. You sent her up the river, remember?

ADAM. So what? You didn't abandon me, and I had most of you killed off.

RITA. Well, we weren't in love with you. She was in love with you and you broke her heart. I doubt she'll ever come back and I can't really blame her.

ADAM. Look, I had to finish the book. Why can't she see that?

ROY. Obviously some people take betrayal personally. Besides, just because we're still hanging around doesn't mean we're all that happy with you. I could have gone to Paris, killed my wife and been rolling in dough. But no, you went and knocked me off at the beginning of the book. I'm the last guy to feel sorry for you.

ADAM. I had a different relationship with Laura. She was special. She wasn't like anyone I ever wrote before. When I was with her, I wasn't lonely. Now every minute away from her is living agony. I blew it. I loved her and I blew it. And for what? For a goddamn book that's never going to be published.

COSLOW. Let it go, Adam. You did what you needed to do. You'd think by now you'd have learned that the last thing a writer should do is fall in love with his characters.

ADAM. Well, I did, okay? I did. That goddamn book didn't have a happy ending and now my life isn't going to have one either.

JOHNNY. What if you started drinking?

ROY. Yeah. Ernest Hemmingway drank.

COSLOW. But he killed himself.

JOHNNY. Exactly.

RITA. Maybe you just need sex. That always seems to cheer guys up.

ADAM. No. I'm finished. I'm throwing in the towel. Plain and simple, I quit.

COSLOW. That's stupid, Adam. You're a writer. As long as you have a laptop, a printer and several reams of paper there's always a chance you'll come up with something that will change your whole world.

ADAM. Like what?

COSLOW. How should I know? You're the creative one. I'm just a poorly written New York Detective, remember? But don't give up because then for sure you'll have nothing.

(The doorbell rings.)

ADAM. Please let it not be my landlord again.

*(**ADAM** rises, goes to the door and opens it. It's **LAURA**, finally and obviously dressed in another outfit. She carries a briefcase.)*

LAURA. Adam Webster?

ADAM. Laura!

LAURA. Uh, no. I'm Amy Tyler. I'm with the Burton and Cobb publishing company. May I come in?

*(Before he can answer she enters the apartment. **ADAM**, stunned, closes the door and follows her. She is oblivious to all but **ADAM**.)*

ADAM. You're not Laura?

LAURA. No. But that's okay. I've been told that I have the kind of face that reminds people of other people. First let me apologize for not calling. I tried but apparently your phone's been disconnected.

*(**ADAM**, **RITA**, **ROY**, **JOHNNY**, and **COSLOW** all turn towards the phone.)*

ADAM. Oh? Maybe that's why it hasn't been ringing.

LAURA. Well, I hope another publisher hasn't beaten me to it, but, Mr. Webster, Burton and Cobb wants to publish your book.

ADAM. "The Psychic"?

JOHNNY. I'll be damned.

LAURA. Everyone at the company was ecstatic over it. Especially the romantic relationship. It actually gave me chills. The sensitivity, the pain, the excruciating decision the hero had to make at the end, to turn in someone he loved. I'll be honest, I've read hundreds of mystery manuscripts. This is the first one that actually made me cry.

ADAM. It did?

JOHNNY. I'll be damned.

LAURA. You're a wonderful writer, Mr. Webster. Absolutely wonderful.

ADAM. I am?

JOHNNY. I'll be goddamned.

LAURA. You most definitely are. We think your book is going to rank right up there with *The Maltese Falcon*. Anyway, we're prepared to give you a hundred thousand dollar advance against ten percent of the net. How does that sound to you?

ADAM. Unreal.

LAURA. I know. Very few writers get anywhere near that good a deal. I hope this won't embarrass you, Mr. Webster, but while reading your book, I was so moved by it, I actually felt a very deep...deep...

ROY, RITA, COSLOW & JOHNNY. Yes?

LAURA. ...connection between us, a peculiar bond of some kind, some sort of previous attachment between us and I have no idea why. That's never happened to me before. Isn't that bizarre?

ADAM. Yes. Very.

(*suspicious*)

Would you do me a big favor Miss...Miss...

LAURA. Tyler. Amy Tyler.

ADAM. Yes. I know this is going to sound crazy but would you let me kiss you, Amy Tyler?

LAURA. Well, I....

(Before she has a chance to resist, he kisses her softly on the lips.)

That really was out of line, Mr. Webster...

ADAM. I know.

LAURA. ...but oddly enough I really didn't mind it.

ADAM. Good. I'd like to do it again.

(He kisses her softly on the lips once more.)

JOHNNY. I have to admit, this I did not expect.

RITA. I love it. It's so romantic.

ROY. Believe it or not, I sort of like it too.

COSLOW. Well, two's company, six is definitely a crowd. Let's go.

(They start out.)

ADAM. *(He turns to the group.)* Hey, guys. Tell me the truth. Is she real or not?

LAURA. Excuse me, but who are you talking to?

ADAM. You don't see anyone?

LAURA. No. No one at all.

ADAM. No one? How wonderful is that?

*(**RITA**, **ROY** and **COSLOW** exit. **JOHNNY** stops at the door.)*

JOHNNY. So long, Adam. This time don't screw it up.

*(**JOHNNY** exits, closing the door behind him.)*

ADAM. Don't worry. I won't.

LAURA. *(puzzled)* What did you say?

ADAM. Nothing. Nothing at all.

*(**ADAM** kisses **LAURA** once more. This is a more passionate kiss. After the kiss, **LAURA** looks at **ADAM** lovingly and smiles.)*

LAURA. Oh, Adam. I like this ending so much better. Don't you?

(**ADAM,** *about to kiss her once more, stops and reacts. Not knowing whether the moment is real or not, he shrugs his shoulders and, happy to go along with whatever it is, kisses her again as the lights slowly fade.*)

The End

COSTUME PLOT

Act	Scene	Character	Costume
I	1	Adam Webster	Jeans, long-sleeve T-shirt with a long-sleeve shirt worn over the T-shirt but left unbuttoned.
I	1	Laura Benson	Pale blue conservative designer suit with a skirt and blouse. Matching tasteful pumps and flesh tone pantyhose. Simple pearl necklace and earrings.
I	2	Adam Webster	Same as previous scene, but without the long-sleeve shirt. Sleeves of the long-sleeve T-shirt are pushed up.
I	2	Roy Benson	Light colored suit and shirt with tie worn loosely tied.
I	3	Adam Webster	Same
I	3	Rita Malone	Very feminine dress with matching high heels. NOTE: She should look sensuous, but not like a Hooker.
I	4	Adam Webster	Jeans and short-sleeve T-shirt. He puts on a different long-sleeve shirt, over the T-shirt, during the scene.
I	4	Laura Benson	Same as in Scene 1, though her suit jacket is hanging on the back of the desk chair.
I	5	Adam Webster	Same
I	5	Laura Benson	Same
I	5	Johnny Bubbles	Dressed like a typical gangster from a 1940's movie. Dark suit (black or blue), vest, dark shirt (burgundy), dark shiny tie, wide brim hat and pinky ring.
I	5	Detective Coslow	Brown suit with lighter shade of brown shirt. Brown tie. Handkerchief in pants pocket.
II	1	Adam Webster	Same
II	1	Laura Benson	Same
II	1	Johnny Bubbles	Same

Act	Scene	Character	Costume
II	1	Detective Coslow	Same
II	2	Adam Webster	Jeans and a different long-sleeve shirt.
II	2	Laura Benson	Same, suit jacket is on.
II	2	Detective Coslow	Same
II	3	Laura Benson	Same, (no jacket) with an apron
II	3	Johnny Bubbles	Same
II	3	Adam Webster	Jeans, different T-shirt with different long-sleeve shirt over and left unbuttoned.
II	4	Adam Webster	Same
II	4	Laura Benson	Same
II	4	Detective Coslow	Same
II	5	Roy Benson	Same
II	5	Johnny Bubbles	Same
II	5	Detective Coslow	Same
II	5	Rita Malone	Same
II	5	Adam Webster	Jeans, different long-sleeve shirt and corduroy sport coat.
II	5	Laura Benson	Hot pink or red suit with skirt, blouse, matching pumps, flesh-tone pantyhose, simple earrings and necklace, but not pearls.

PROP PLOT

Act	Scene	Character	Item	Notes
I	1	Adam	Laptop computer	On desk
I	1	Adam	Printer	Small, desk size – placed on top of four foot high bookcase adjacent to Adam's desk
I	1	Adam	Telephone	On desk
I	1	Adam	Yellow lined notepad	On desk
I	1	Adam	Pencil	On desk
I	1	Adam	Sign: Psychic Readings $25	Sturdy cardboard, written in crayon, placed in window
I	1	Adam	Stack of business cards	Placed on Adam's desk. Some written in ink, some written in pencil.
I	1	Laura	Purse	Expensive looking
I	1	Laura	Wallet	Stored in her purse
I	1	Laura	Money	Three tens
I	1	Adam	Wallet	Three ones
I	1	Adam	Small dish with coins	Six quarters, two dimes, four nickels and ten pennies
I	1	Adam	Deck of tarot cards	Brand new, unopened package
I	2	Roy	Adam's business card	Written in pencil
I	2	Roy	Several type written pages	From Adam's desk
I	2	Roy	Wallet with money	Three $10 bills
I	3	Rita	Purse	Big enough to fit a handgun
I	3	Rita	Powder compact	Stored in her purse
I	3	Rita	Hair brush	Stored in her purse
I	3	Rita	Handgun	Stored in her purse
I	3	Rita	Wallet or pouch with money	Two $10 bills, one $5 bill

Act	Scene	Character	Item	Notes
I	4	Laura	Several type written pages	From Adam's story: the progress
I	4	Adam	Laundry basket with clothes	Adam's clean, folded clothes
I	4	Adam	Coffee maker/ clear carafe/ coffee	Coffee is Coke
I	4	Adam/ Laura	Coffee mugs	
I	5	Johnny	Handgun	Stored in his inside jacket pocket
I	5	Johnny	Toothpicks	Stored in his vest pocket
I	5	Detective Coslow	NYPD Detective badge	In wallet-type holder
I	5	Detective Coslow	Adam's business card	In small clear Evidence bag The word "Evidence" is stenciled on the clear bag in red letters. Stored in other jacket pocket.
II	1	Detective Coslow	Reading glasses	Stored in his shirt pocket
II	1	Detective Coslow	Several type written pages	Adam's story
II	1	Detective Coslow	Small notebook	Spiral bound at top, stored in his jacket pocket
II	1	Detective Coslow	Pen	Stored with the notebook
II	1	Detective Coslow	Cell phone	Flip open style with 'O Solo Mio" ringtone
II	2	Detective Coslow	Adam's business card	In small clear evidence bag. The word "Evidence" is stenciled on the clear bag in red letters. Stored in other jacket pocket.
II	3	Laura	Metal mixing bowl	

Act	Scene	Character	Item	Notes
II	3	Laura	Metal whisk	
II	3	Laura	A type written page	Placed in the printer output tray
II	3	Adam	NY newspaper	Carries it as he enters
II	4	Detective Coslow	Pair of hand-cuffs	
II	5	Adam	Stack of 8 ½ x 11 manila envelopes containing rejected manuscripts	On desk
II	5	Adam	Stack of manu-scripts	On desk, rejected
II	5	Detective Coslow	Coffee maker, clear carafe & coffee	Coffee is Coke
II	5	Detective Coslow	Several coffee mugs	
II	5	Adam	Five 8 ½ x 11 manila enve-lopes	Rejected manuscripts he carries in.
II	5	Detective Coslow	Several reams of paper	Indicated, on bookcase shelf
II	5	Laura	Briefcase	As Amy, the publisher

The Psychic

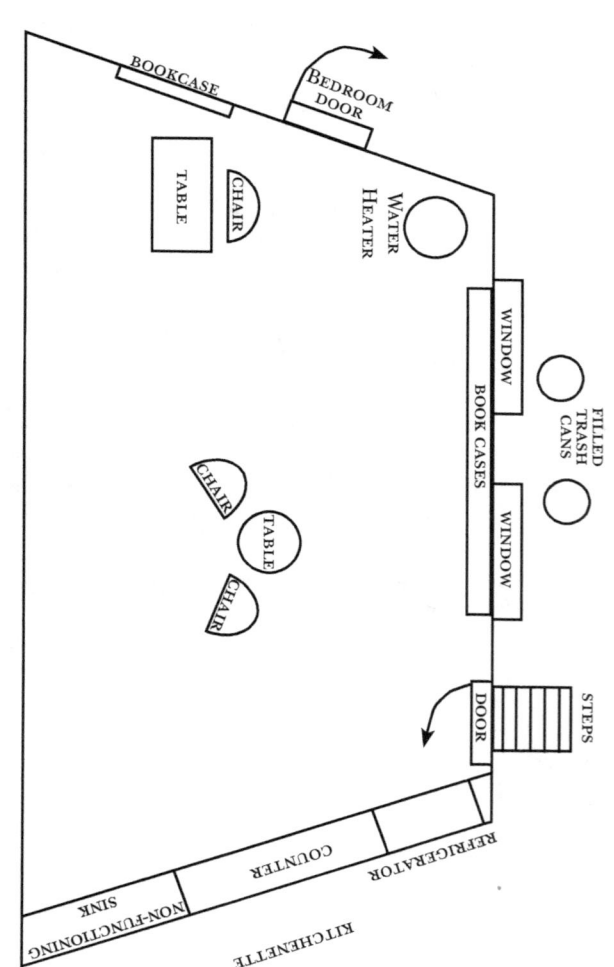

Also by
Sam Bobrick...

Annoyance

Are You Sure?

Baggage

The Crazy Time

Death in England

Flemming (An American Thriller)

Getting Sara Married

Hamlet II

Last Chance Romance

Murder at the Howard Johnson's

New York Water

No Hard Feelings

Norman, is that You?

**The Outrageous Adventures of
Sheldon & Mrs. Levine**

Passengers

RememberMe?

**Splitting Issues
(And Other Noteworthy Concerns)**

The Stanway Case

Wally's Cafe

Weekend Comedy

Please visit our website **samuelfrench.com** for complete
descriptions and licensing information.